Questions and Answers: Countries

Haiti

A Question and Answer Book

by June Preszler

Consultant:
Robert Maguire
Director, Haiti Program
Trinity University, Washington, D.C.

Capstone press

Mankato, Minnesota

Fact Finders is published by Capstone Press
151 Good Counsel Drive, P.O. Box 669, Mankato, Minnesota 56002.
www.capstonepress.com

Library of Congress Cataloging-in-Publication Data
Preszler, June, 1954–
    Haiti : a question and answer book / by June Preszler.
    p. cm.—(Questions and answers. Countries)
    Includes bibliographical references and index.
    ISBN–13: 978–0–7368–6770–2 (hardcover)
    ISBN–10: 0–7368–6770–8 (hardcover)
    1. Haiti—Juvenile literature. 2. Haiti—Miscellanea. I. Title. II. Series.
F1915.2.P74 2007
972.94—dc22   2006028236

Summary: Describes the geography, history, economy, and culture of Haiti in a
    question-and-answer format.

Editorial Credits
Silver Editions, editorial, design, photo research and production; Kia Adams, set designer;
    Maps.com, cartographer

Photo Credits
AP/Wide World Photos/Ariana Cubillos, 23; Daniel Morel, 15
Art Resource, NY/Manu Sassoonian, 21
Bruce Coleman Inc./Candace Scharsu, 11
Capstone Press Archives, 29 (money)
Corbis/Owen Franken, cover (foreground); Paul A. Souders, 27; photocuisine, 25
Getty Images Inc./AFP/Roberto Schmidt, 19; Thony Belizaire, 9
The Granger Collection, New York, 7
The Image Works/Sean Sprague, 17
Index Stock Imagery/Michele Burgess, 13; Murray Sill, cover (background)
One Mile Up, Inc., 29 (flag)
SuperStock, Inc., 1; Michele Burgess, 4

1 2 3 4 5 6 12 11 10 09 08 07

Table of Contents

Where is Haiti? 4

When did Haiti become a country? 6

What type of government does Haiti have? 8

What kind of housing does Haiti have? 10

What are Haiti's forms of transportation? 12

What are Haiti's major industries? 14

What is school like in Haiti? 16

What are Haiti's favorite sports and games? 18

What are the traditional art forms in Haiti? 20

What holidays do people in Haiti celebrate? 22

What are the traditional foods of Haiti? 24

What is family life like in Haiti? 26

Features

Haiti Fast Facts 28

Money and Flag 29

Learn to Speak Creole 30

Glossary 30

Internet Sites 31

Read More 31

Index 32

Where is Haiti?

Haiti shares the island of Hispaniola with the Dominican Republic. Haiti takes up the western part of the island. The country is no bigger than the U.S. state of Maryland.

Hispaniola is located between the Caribbean Sea and the Atlantic Ocean. It has a hot, **humid** climate. **Hurricanes** commonly hit the island.

Mountains border the coastline at Cap-Haïtien.

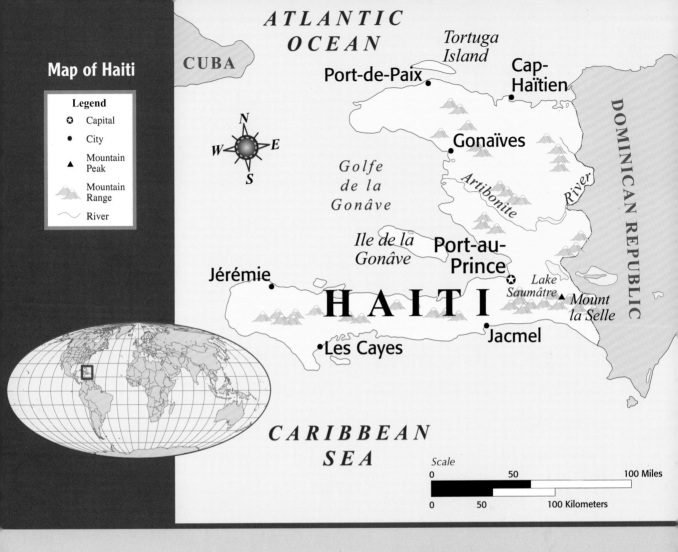

Map of Haiti

Legend
- ⊕ Capital
- • City
- ▲ Mountain Peak
- Mountain Range
- River

ATLANTIC OCEAN

CUBA

Tortuga Island

Port-de-Paix

Cap-Haïtien

Gonaïves

DOMINICAN REPUBLIC

Golfe de la Gonâve

Artibonite River

Ile de la Gonâve

Port-au-Prince

Jérémie

Lake Saumâtre

▲ Mount la Selle

HAITI

Jacmel

•Les Cayes

CARIBBEAN SEA

Scale
0 ——— 50 ——— 100 Miles
0 ——— 50 ——— 100 Kilometers

Mountains cover most of Haiti's 10,714 square miles (27,750 square kilometers). Valleys, plateaus, and plains cover the rest of Haiti's land. Haiti also includes two smaller islands, Tortuga and la Gonâve.

When did Haiti become a country?

Haiti became an independent **republic** in 1804. Before that, it was a colony of first Spain, then France.

The French brought African slaves to work on their island plantations. By 1791, the slaves had grown tired of poor treatment. They rose up against the French and defeated them. Haiti became the world's first free, black republic in 1804.

Fact!

The name Haiti came from the Arawak Indians, who were living on Hispaniola when Christopher Columbus claimed it for Spain in 1492. Haiti means "land of mountains."

Toussaint L'Ouverture (center) led slaves to fight for their rights and freedom from the French.

The country has had periods of unrest since its beginning. Civil war, killings of government leaders, and military takeovers have kept government unstable. Today, Haiti's government still faces unrest.

What type of government does Haiti have?

Today, Haiti is a republic. People who are at least 18 years old can vote. Like the United States, Haiti's government has three branches. They are the executive, the legislative, and the judicial branches.

Haitians elect a president to lead the country. The president appoints a prime minister to run the government. The legislative branch is made up of the Senate and the Chamber of Deputies.

Fact!

Although many Haitians who now live as citizens in the United States and Canada would like to vote in Haiti's elections, their native country's constitution won't let them.

President René Préval listens to the comments and concerns of his fellow Haitians.

Most Haitians want to live peacefully. Even so, their history is full of unrest. In 2004, protesters forced President Jean-Bertrand Aristide to leave the country. Two years later, Haitians elected René Préval to be president.

What kind of housing does Haiti have?

About 80 percent of Haitians live in **poverty**. The average worker makes $300 a year. Most people cannot afford expensive homes. Many of the poor people in Haiti's cities live in shacks or very simple homes. Shacks are often made of cardboard, plastic, or tin.

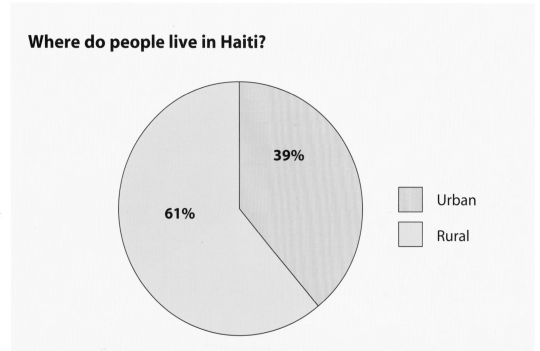

Where do people live in Haiti?

39%

61%

Urban

Rural

Homes in Haiti may be made of simple, brightly painted materials.

People who live in nicer homes usually have only two or three rooms. In most homes, the kitchen is separate from the rest of the house. In the countryside, the kitchen may even be outside. This setup keeps the house from getting hot when the family cooks.

What are Haiti's forms of transportation?

Most Haitians cannot afford cars. Instead, many people walk or ride bikes from place to place. Rural Haitians rely on animals, such as donkeys, to carry goods.

Buses, taxis, and other forms of public transportation are also popular. People crowd into colorfully painted buses called tap-taps. You tap on the window to let the driver know when you want to get off. Ferries carry people and goods between coastal cities.

Fact!

Some of the buses in Haiti were once used for school children in the United States.

A fleet of colorful tap-taps carries passengers in Port-au-Prince.

As part of an island, Haiti relies on planes and ships for travel and trade with other countries. Haiti has many ports along its coast. It's largest is at Cap-Haïtien. Haiti has 13 airports, but only a few have paved runways. Port-au-Prince contains the largest international airport.

What are Haiti's major industries?

In Haiti, many people do not have steady jobs. Two-thirds of those with jobs work on farms. Farmers grow corn, rice, beans, peanuts, and fruit to feed their families. They also grow coffee, cocoa, sugarcane, and mangoes to sell to other countries.

About 25 percent of Haitians work in the service industry. This work includes government, tourism, and teaching jobs. These jobs often pay more than farm work.

What does Haiti import and export?

Imports	Exports
food	assembled goods
petroleum products	coffee
manufactured goods	mangoes
raw material	cocoa

Farms in Haiti produce coffee beans that are sold to countries around the world.

Factory workers in Haiti usually earn less than $3.00 a day. Workers in Port-au-Prince might make sporting goods, electronics, or clothing. Other workers produce food, cement, detergent, flour, and soap.

What is school like in Haiti?

Haiti's school system consists of primary and secondary school. Students ages 7 to 13 attend primary school. They study reading, writing, history, math, and science. They also learn French and Creole languages.

Students take a test at the end of primary to move on to secondary school. Secondary school has two parts. The first is like the upper grades in U.S. high schools. The second is more like college.

Fact!

Only 53 percent of Haitians can read and write. The good news is that literacy is improving among Haiti's young people. In the last 25 years, literacy among people ages 15 to 24 has risen by at least 20 percent.

In recent years, more students than ever before are learning to read in Haiti's schools.

By law, public school is free in Haiti. Parents must pay for uniforms and supplies. These costs keep many children from school.

Haiti also has a shortage of public schools. In the countryside, there are few, if any, secondary schools.

What are Haiti's favorite sports and games?

Soccer is Haiti's national sport. Almost all Haitian boys play soccer. They play on fields or on the city streets. Haiti's national soccer team competes against other teams from the Caribbean. Their matches attract huge crowds to the Sylvio Cator Stadium in Port-au-Prince.

Haitian children also enjoy hopscotch, tag, and kite flying. They know how to make fun toys out of common items, such as string and pieces of wood or cloth.

Fact!

Haiti first competed in the World Cup soccer competition in 1974.

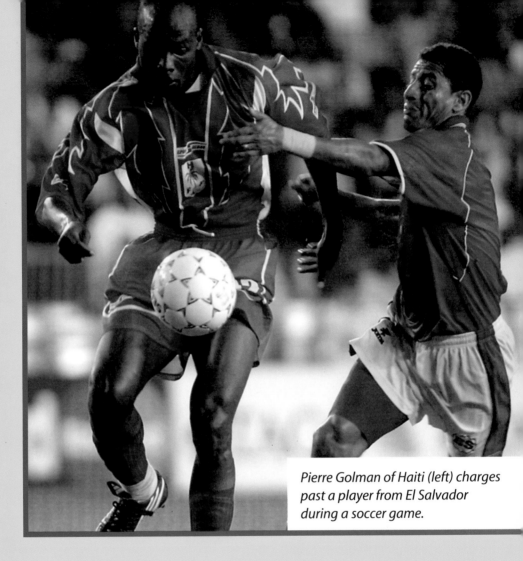

Pierre Golman of Haiti (left) charges past a player from El Salvador during a soccer game.

Because Haiti is on a tropical island, many people know how to swim, dive, and sail. Tourists from all over also enjoy Haiti's beautiful forests and beaches.

What are the traditional art forms in Haiti?

Much of Haiti's art comes from paintings found in Voodoo temples. Voodoo is a religion from Africa practiced by many Haitians. Paintings and drawings often show all kinds of animals and spirits.

Today, Haitian artists show everyday life in their works. Bright colors appear in most of their crafts.

Fact!

The popular Haitian band Boukman Eksperyans is named after a leader from the slave revolts in Haiti's history.

This colorful painting depicts a celebration during Carnival in Cap-Haïtien.

Music and dance in Haiti also have close ties to religion. Both are common in celebrations and rituals. Two forms of popular dance music are called *compas* and *rara*. Today's "roots" music in Haiti adds elements of soul, funk, jazz, and rap.

What holidays do people in Haiti celebrate?

Several Haitian holidays honor important dates in Haiti's history. January 1 marks the day in 1804 when Haiti became the first black republic in the world.

Haiti also celebrates many Christian holidays. Just before Lent, people celebrate Carnival. They take part in parades, parties, and dances. In many ways, Carnival is like Mardi Gras in New Orleans.

What other holidays do people in Haiti celebrate?

Ancestors' Day
Flag and University Day
United Nations Day
All Saints Day
Christmas Day

Music and dance are important parts of many holiday celebrations in Haiti, especially Carnival.

After Carnival, many people listen to *rara* bands. These Voodoo groups travel around the country. They dance, sing, beat drums, and play all kinds of instruments. Some *rara* bands can include hundreds of musicians.

What are the traditional foods of Haiti?

Haitian meals often have a base of rice, beans, corn, **cassava**, or **millet**. When they can afford it, Haitians add meat, fish, or eggs to their meals.

Good fruit is easy to find in this **tropical** country. Bananas, mangoes, oranges, and grapefruit all grow well in Haiti.

Haitians use many spices to make their foods tasty. Their famous Creole dishes mix French, African, and Haitian flavors. Griot is a special meal that mixes fried pork with a spicy sauce.

Fact!

Haitians enjoy eating locally-produced spaghetti, sometimes fried up for breakfast.

Many spicy dishes in Haiti are served over a bed of steaming rice.

Haiti's favorite drinks come from plants grown on the island. Many adults drink coffee. Fruit juices are popular with everyone. Local people use sugarcane to make a very sweet cola drink that kids love.

What is family life like in Haiti?

Until the mid-1900s, most rural Haitians lived in large family groups called *lakou*. Everyone in the *lakou* worked together and cared for each other.

Today, many people live and work in cities. Most families include just parents and children. More women have jobs than before.

What are the ethnic backgrounds of people in Haiti?

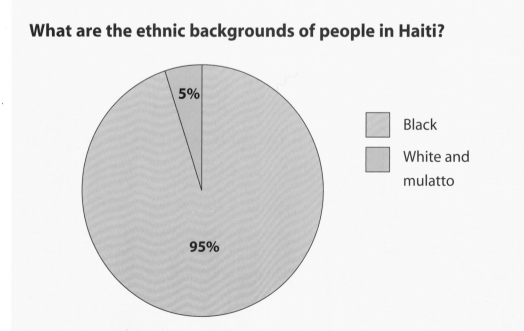

5%

95%

Black

White and mulatto

Even though more young women now work outside the home, they take great pride in raising their children.

Many Haitians have also moved to other countries. It is common to have family members living in the United States and Canada. These relatives often send money back home. This shows that no matter where Haitians live, their family ties remain strong.

Haiti Fast Facts

Official name:

Republic of Haiti

Land area:

*10,714 square miles
(27,750 square kilometers)*

**Average annual
precipitation
(Port-au-Prince):**

53 inches (135 centimeters)

**Average
January temperature:**

*77 degrees Fahrenheit
(25 degrees Celsius)*

**Average
July temperature:**

*84 degrees Fahrenheit
(29 degrees Celsius)*

Population:

8,100,000 people

Capital city:

Port-au-Prince

Languages:

French and Creole

Natural resources:

*wood, bauxite, copper, gold,
construction materials, gravel,
limestone*

Religions:

Roman Catholic	*80%*
Protestant	*16%*
Voodoo	***
Other	*4%*

**statistics not available; Voodoo is
often practiced alongside Christianity.*

Money and Flag

Money:

Haiti's money is called the gourde. One gourde equals 100 centimes. In July 2006, one U.S. dollar equaled 39 Haitian gourdes. One Canadian dollar equaled about 36 Haitian gourdes.

Flag:

The Haitian flag has two horizontal bands. The band on top is blue and the bottom band is red. Haiti's coat of arms appears in a white rectangle in the center. It features a palm tree, two cannons, and the motto "L'Union Fait La Force," which means "Union Makes Strength."

Learn to Speak Creole

Creole and French are the two official languages of Haiti. Most Haitians speak Creole as their primary language. Learn to speak some Creole words and phrases below.

English	Creole	Pronunciation
yes	wi	WEE
no	non	NOHN
thank you	mesi anpil	MEH-si ahn-PIHL
stop	rete	REH-tay
good morning	bonjou	bohn-ZHOO
good evening	bonswa	bohn-SWAH
good-bye	m'ale	muh-LAY
how are you	sak pase	SAHK puh-SAY

Glossary

cassava (kuh-SAH-vuh)—a starchy plant used as the basis for tapioca

humid (HYOO-muhd)—damp and moist

hurricane (HUH-ruh-kayn)—a tropical storm with high winds and heavy rainfall

millet (MI-luht)—grain used for food

poverty (PAW-vuhr-tee)—the state of being poor or without money

republic (ree-PUHB-lik)—a government headed by a president with officials elected by the people

tropical (TRAH-pi-kuhl)—of or near the equator; in weather, hot and humid

Voodoo (VOO-doo)—a religion that began in Africa; Voodoo is also spelled Vodou.

Internet Sites

FactHound offers a safe, fun way to find Internet sites related to this book. All of the sites on FactHound have been researched by our staff.

Here's how:
1. Visit *www.facthound.com*
2. Choose your grade level.
3. Type in this book ID **0736867708** for age-appropriate sites. You may also browse subjects by clicking on letters, or by clicking on pictures and words.
4. Click on the **Fetch It** button.

FactHound will fetch the best sites for you!

Read More

Brown-Carpenter, Katharine, and Michele Wagner. *Welcome to Haiti.* Welcome to My Country. Milwaukee: Gareth Stevens, 2003.

Dell'Oro, Suzanne Paul. *Haiti.* Countries of the World. Mankato, Minn.: Bridgestone Books, 2002.

Goldstein, Margaret J. *Haiti in Pictures.* Visual Geography Series. Minneapolis: Lerner, 2006.

Wagner, Michele. *Haiti.* Countries of the World. Milwaukee: Gareth Stevens, 2002.

Index

agriculture, 14, 15, 24, 25
Aristide, Jean-Bertrand, 9
art, 20–21

Canada, 8, 27
capital. *See* Port-au-Prince
Carnival, 21, 22, 23
climate, 4, 19, 24, 28
Columbus, Christopher, 6
compas, 21
Creole, 16, 28, 30

education, 16–17
ethnic groups, 26
exports, 14–15

family life, 26–27
farming. *See* agriculture
flag, 29
food, 24–25
France, 6

games, 18–19
government, 6–7, 8–9, 14
griot, 23

holidays, 22–23
housing, 10–11

imports, 14
independence, 6–7, 22, 23
industries, 14–15

lakou, 26
landforms, 4–5
languages, 16, 28, 30

money, 29
music, 21, 23

natural resources, 28

population, 26, 28
Port-au-Prince, 13, 15, 28
Préval, René, 9

rara, 21, 23
religion, 20, 21, 23, 28

schools. *See* education
soccer, 18, 19
Spain, 6
sports, 18–19

tap-taps, 12, 13
tourism, 14, 19
transportation, 12–13

United States, 8, 12, 27

Voodoo, 20, 23

weather. *See* climate